FUNNY

stories

D0620641

Look out for other exciting stories
in the *Shades Shorts* series:

FUNNY
stories

Gillian Philip
Alan Durant
Alex Stewart
Julia Williams

Published by Evans Brothers Limited
2A Portman Mansions
Chiltern St
London W1U 6NR

Shades Shorts: Funny Stories © Evans Brothers Limited 2009
The Kindest Cut © 2009 Gillian Philip
Jez Fisher and the Case of the Cocky Robin © 2009 Alan Durant
Asking Andrea © 2009 Alex Stewart
A Dish Best Served Cold © 2009 Julia Williams

First published in 2009

All rights reserved. No part of this publication
may be reproduced, stored in a retrieval system
or transmitted in any form, or by any means,
electronic, mechanical, photocopying, recording
or otherwise, without the prior permission of
Evans Brothers Limited.

British Library Cataloguing in Publication Data
 Funny stories.. -- (Shades shorts)
   1. Humorous stories, English. 2. Young adult fiction,
   English.
   I. Series II. Philip, Gillian, 1964-
   823'.010817-dc22

 ISBN-13: 9780237539436

Editor: Julia Moffatt
Designer: Rob Walster

Contents

The
Kindest
Cut

The Kindest Cut

by Gillian Philip

I slouched behind Mum as she marched across the car park, bearing a livid ginger tom like a blood sacrifice. Neither of us was ever going to speak to her again.

'You didn't have to come along,' she told me. 'You did,' she added to the tom, which was swishing its tail malevolently against the KittyKarry.

'I wouldn't leave him alone at a time

like this.'

'What's this? Male solidarity? I knew it. Do you spend all your time at your father's watching Sky Sports? Does he let you drink lager? Do you vet his *girlfriends?*'

She was in some mood. Shoving through the glass doors into the surgery, she banged the KittyKarry accidentally (I think). Potatoface yowled with hatred.

'Mum.' I tried the soft-soap approach. 'It isn't too late. We can talk about this.'

The soft soap must have reminded her of Dad. She bristled.

'Potatoface is a proud father several times over. We are neighbourhood pariahs. This is the kindest thing. He'll be a happier cat. He'll settle down. He'll be more ... affectionate.'

'Mum.' I gave her my finest inherited stare. 'Is this a feminist thing?'

'That's it,' she snapped. 'I am rethinking your father's weekend access. This is a *humane* thing. Ask the vet.'

I couldn't.

'He's just popped out,' said the receptionist. 'Hi, kitty. Clark, isn't it?'

She was new, the receptionist. Looked almost younger than me, and I could see dried spot cream on her chin. The lines from Mum's fixed smile were etching themselves into her face. Under her breath she muttered, 'Correct, Lolita.'

I coughed to drown her out.

'Potatoface Clark,' I told the girl.

'Clark, Potatoface. Here we are.' She tapped her keyboard. 'He's due for this.'

'Long overdue.' Mum gave me a triumphant glance, but I rubbed Potatoface's nose through the mesh.

'Poor old cat. Mum's never liked you.

You should have gone with Dad, but it wouldn't have been fair to upset your environment.'

Now, that was working the guilt trip as hard as it would go. Mum's face started to crumple.

'Zack, darling...'

'Your mum's doing the right thing,' said Lolita.

I gave her a glower.

'Thank you,' Mum told her, heaving the spitting Potatoface on to the counter.

One last try. I spread my arms in front of the KittyKarry.

'Mum. Have you ever heard of emotional projection?'

'I'm taking you out of that school.'

'They're getting a divorce,' I explained to the bemused Lolita. 'It's very acrimonious.'

'Please excuse my son,' said Mum. 'It's his genes. Let's go, Zack.'

'But Mum, can't we even wait and say good—'

'ZACK!'

'Okay. If you can live with yourself.'

'As if I have another option.' She was actually starting to sniffle. 'And stop looking at me with those big blue eyes.'

What? Like I could change them for her brown ones?

'Sorry, Dad. It was Mum's idea.'

'No worries.' He gave Mum a rueful smile as he hovered on the doorstep. 'It was a good one.'

Mum had lost that smug look she'd worn since picking up Potatoface this morning.

'Mister Rational,' she muttered.

'I should have done it ages ago,' Dad went

on. 'Feels a bit final, though, doesn't it?'

Not as final as it did for Potatoface. Oh, it was all very symbolic. Sort of a premature Decree Absolute.

'He's happy to be home.' Dad looked half ironic, half wistful as he stroked the subdued Potatoface. He'd like to come home himself, he'd told me. But Mum wasn't having it. 'He'll stay home now, too. Won't go tomcatting around, will you, mate?'

'*Rowl*,' said Potatoface miserably.

'Zack, get your coat,' Mum said briskly. 'Don't keep your father waiting.'

Dad headed for his car, his jacket unfastened and his hair all wind-rumpled.

I picked up my coat.

'He doesn't look well, Mum. He's a mess.'

'His mess,' she said briskly. 'My life's very neat and tidy now. I don't want your father leaving his dirty socks all over it.

Metaphorically speaking.'

It was six months since she'd thrown him out. His first affair in twelve years was apparently going to be his only one, because Mum wasn't giving him the chance to do it twice.

He'd told her the whole thing had been a stupid infatuation, but Mum said coming a distant second to a stupid infatuation wasn't the most flattering thing that had ever happened to her.

He said he was sorry and Mum believed him. He said it wouldn't happen again, but Mum didn't believe that bit.

Lolita was walking away from the vet's as I walked in; the surgery was shut. Light still spilled from the windows onto the gravel, though.

The glass door was locked but he was

standing just inside, flicking through a file, gloves between his teeth. When I rattled the door, he looked up and grinned at me, took the gloves out of his mouth and undid the lock.

'Hi, Zack! What's up?'

'Potatoface.' I panted for breath, quite convincingly. 'He's very sick. You have to come.'

'*What?* Why didn't your mother call?'

'Are you *kidding?*' I leaned on the counter and gave my father his own withering look. 'She thinks it's the op. She's devastated by guilt. Blaming herself. Didn't want to tell you.'

'Oh?' He was looking a bit sceptical, so I had to regroup a little.

'She's emotionally confused. Whose fault is that?'

That ought to do it.

'You barefaced liar,' said my father, as Potatoface shot through the kitchen catflap into his arms. 'This cat is fine.'

'This cat is sick. Mum said so this morning, when he brought her a crippled mouse to play with. She screamed and said, "*You're a sick little—*" '

'That's enough. See you. I'm going home.'

'What are you doing here?' That was Mum, of course, walking into the kitchen and nearly falling over. They both glared at me.

'Well, Dad,' I mumbled, kicking the table leg. 'Mum *is* an emotional wreck. She's been mooning over photo albums all week. Your photos. She's even being nice to Potatoface.'

'Don't you talk about me like I'm not here,' said Mum, who had gone vermilion.

'I'll ask you again, Zack: what's he
doing here?'

'Don't talk about *me* as if *I'm* not here,'
pointed out Dad.

'I thought the pair of you might like to
just talk,' I interrupted. 'Instead of swapping
solicitors' letters.'

A hideous and awkward silence fell.
This was going quite well.

'Mum's not so angry any more,' I told
Dad. 'She's worked out her feelings a bit.'

'Remind me *never* to tell you anything
again,' seethed Mum.

Dad stared at his feet. Sometimes he
didn't look any older than me.

'And how is Potatoface doing?'

'Foul as ever.' Mum put her pinkie up to
her eye, catching what looked like a tear.

'Hardest routine neutering I've ever
done.' Dad winced. 'It felt like a penance.'

'No kidding, Sherlock,' I said under my breath.

'He is your cat,' Mum said. 'And you're our vet.'

'Is that all?'

'Well, you're Zack's father too,' said Mum, grudgingly. She was balanced so precariously on her dignity, she looked like she was about to fall off.

'Mum was crying over the Christmas photos,' I told Dad accusingly. 'She was touching your face and going—'

Mum put her hands over her face and swore like a trooper.

'Don't tell tales on your mother,' said Dad. 'That's not acceptable behaviour.'

'Zack's been absolutely impossible,' said Mum, with feeling. 'He gives me a *really hard time*.'

'Yeah? Me too. Every second weekend.'

'He gives you a hard time too? I thought it was me getting all the blame.'

By this time they'd forgotten I was listening.

'You weren't to blame,' said Dad. 'You had every right to be angry.'

'Yes. But I might—' Mum looked at the shoulder of Dad's waxed jacket. 'I might have been a little extreme.'

'You didn't overreact, really—'

'I didn't say I overreacted!' she yelled. 'Just that ... deciding what I want ... I've been a little ... *extreme*.'

He rubbed his hair. 'So, erm ... what *do* you want?'

She gave him a faint smile. 'I don't know really. Not any more.'

He said seriously, 'That's a start. Isn't it?'

'Might be. Oh, my solicitor's going to *kill* me.'

His old familiar grin was broad and crinkly, but he managed eventually to subdue it.

'No promises,' she warned.

'Except I promise no more, erm ... tomcatting.'

'Whoa, cowboy. This might not work. It's just a chance, that's all.'

'I'll take that.'

She grunted. 'Sorry about Potatoface.'

Dad grinned. 'I'm not.'

I waited till she showed him to the front door, where they seemed to linger for a long time. Then I sneaked back into the kitchen and burgled the freezer. I could take the packet to my room and defrost it. Mum would never miss it. She was emotionally confused.

Poor Potatoface had made the ultimate sacrifice. Smoked salmon was the least I could do.

Jez Fisher and the Case of the Cocky Robin

Jez Fisher and the Case of the Cocky Robin

by Alan Durant

My name is Fisher, Jez Fisher. I'm a boy detective. My speciality? The weird and bizarre. Check this out.

My first client is a robin.

'My name's Peter,' he tweets, 'and I've got a problem. A cat problem.'

'A cat problem?'

'Yeah. This cat's giving me grief. I want her off my tail. Will you take the case?'

'Can you afford me?' I ask.

'How much do you charge?'

'Fifty pounds a day plus expenses.'

'Hmmm,' he muses. 'How about some stale lardy cake and a bacon rind? With a few holly berries thrown in.'

I shrug. Times are hard.

'I'll take the case,' I say.

I arrive at the cat's house and walk up to the door. There's no knocker or bell, just a cord dangling down. I pull, setting off a tinkly chorus of 'Hi, ho! Hi, ho! It's off to work we go...'

The door opens and there's no one there.

'You rang,' a voice says.

I look down on a matted bird's nest. Then the nest goes back and a face appears. I am now looking at a dwarf with a wig. That explains the Snow White theme tune.

'My name's Fisher,' I say. 'I'm a private detective. I wonder if I might have a word about your cat.'

'Has she been telling tales again?' asks the dwarf, frowning.

'No,' I say. 'I'm actually here on behalf of a robin.'

'Oh, well,' he says. 'You'd better come in.'

He takes me through to the back room. There are coloured pencils, paints, brushes and paper everywhere. In one corner stands an easel.

'This must be the drawing room,' I say. 'Are you an artist?'

'No,' he says. 'But Leonardo is.'

'Leonardo?'

'The cat,' he replies. 'Her name is Leonardo da Vinci. You may have heard of her. She's a very famous painter.'

'So, Leonardo da Vinci's a cat, eh?'

24

This case is proving to be more complex than I thought.

'May I ask where your cat is now?' I ask.

'Huh!' the dwarf exclaims. 'Making an exhibition of herself somewhere no doubt.'

'Well,' I say. 'While I am waiting for her, do you mind if I take a look around?'

'Be my guest,' he says. 'I have a parrot in the study waiting for his French lesson.'

And with that he departs.

There's something creepy about the room. I feel like I'm being watched. Then I realise what it is. It's the windows. They follow you wherever you go.

'You boys must see everything that goes on around here,' I say.

'But of course, Monsieur Detective, we are ze ice of ze rhume.'

I stare at them, bemused.

'I beg your pardon,' I say.

'We are ze ice of ze rhume,' they repeat, slowly this time.

And then the light dawns. Of course, they are French windows! And the dwarf gives French lessons. The French connection...

'So,' I say. 'If, as you say, you are the eyes of the room, what can you tell me about this Leonardo character?'

'She ees a cat,' they say smugly.

It's time to get tough.

'Now, look here, you greasy fenetres,' I growl. 'I can see right through you, so don't get cute. I want some straight answers and I want them now – or it'll be curtains for you.'

'Ah Monsieur Detective,' they whine, coming over all misty, 'do not be 'ard on us. We 'ave ze pains all over.'

'Ok, quit whimpering,' I order. 'Tell me

what you know about Leonardo and Peter, the robin.'

'Ah, that robin!' they cry. ''E is a scallywag. 'E try to steal Leonardo's paintings.'

Now I see what a cunning rascal this robin is. He comes to my office to hire me to keep a cat off his tail – and the reason this cat is on his tail is because he's an art thief after the cat's paintings. So, while I'm busy with the cat, he makes off with the swag. Some scam. I turn to the curtains.

'What can you guys tell me about this business?' I ask.

But they refuse to be drawn.

I continue my inspection of the room. If Robin Peter is a thief, then he must have some means of access. I peer up the chimney. It's blacker than Humpty Dumpty's bananas. I get the poker and have a poke around. Two things happen. First, I get a face full of soot. Second, a little voice chirps, 'Quit poking me, birdbrain!'

Into the grate tumbles a small angry blackbird. I've never seen such a small blackbird before. But then this bird isn't a blackbird at all as I soon discover: he's a very sooty sparrow.

'I'm sorry,' I apologise. 'I didn't know there was anyone up there. I'm looking for a robin art thief whom I suspect to be operating in this house.'

The sparrow glares at me like I'm an undernourished worm.

'Well he would be, wouldn't he?'

'Would be what?' I enquire.

'Robbin', of course,' says the sparrow. 'That's what thieves do, ain't it?'

'No,' I say, 'I mean the art thief *is* a

robin – Robin Peter.'

'The robin's robbin' Peter?'

'No, the robin *is* Peter. And he's also an art thief.'

'Ah, now I get you, kid,' twitters the sparrow. 'This robin's a criminal, a hood, right?'

'Yeah,' I say. 'You catch on quick.'

'Yeah, well, I only know one Robin Hood and his name ain't Peter.'

'What is his name?' I ask.

'His name's Robin, of course. And he's a real cocky jailbird. Peter must be his alias.'

I sigh deeply. This case has got more twists than a bowl of spaghetti.

Suddenly, the door flips open and the sparrow flies. A sleek blue cat waltzes into the room. She comes in a few paces then stops and licks her delicate whiskers. This is one kitty that definitely gets the cream.

'My name's Fisher, Jez Fisher,' I say. 'You must be Leonardo.'

'No,' she replies. 'I've just eaten, thank you. Now, what can I do for you, young man?'

'Well, Leonardo,' I say, 'this robin comes to my office claiming you're bothering him and asking me to get you off his tail when—'

I get no further. There is a loud and terrible caterwauling and Leonardo throws herself on the floor.

'My painting!' she wails, pointing at the empty easel. 'Someone has stolen my latest painting!'

This discovery cracks the case wide open.

'Can you describe the picture to me?' I ask, when Leonardo has stopped screaming.

She tells me it's a picture of a giant

nose growing up out of the desert. In the background is a man with a French horn and a Spanish smile.

'This discovery cracks the case wide open,' Leonardo declares.

'That's just what I was thinking,' I say.

Leonardo shakes her head. 'No, no. That's the title of the painting.'

I go over to the windows.

'Our frames are sealed,' they say with a glazed expression.

I inspect them anyway. They're locked. But I still don't trust them. 'Keep them covered, chums,' I say to the curtains.

The door opens slowly and the dwarf appears in the doorway.

'Sorry to have kept you,' he says. 'You know the old saying, "You can take a parrot to a study, but you can't make it speak French".'

I don't know this saying, but I nod anyway – a trick I learnt from Mr Noddy, one of the teachers at my old school, who had a very large head. He had big ears too, but that's another story.

The dwarf frowns.

'What's happening here?' he enquires.

'Well, er—' I stop, realising I don't know the dwarf's name.

'Paul,' he says and he gives a little bow. And suddenly everything's as clear as the wig – or toupee – on his head. The case is solved.

'Toupee Paul, right?' I say.

The dwarf looks shaken.

I take a quick step forward, grab hold of his matted toupee and whip it off his head.

There, sitting on the dwarf's bald head, is my startled client.

'So, it's a case of Robin Peter, Toupee Paul,' I say.

'It's a fair cop,' says the robin. 'Got any peanuts?'

I can just make out the man with the French horn, peering out from under the notorious thief's bottom. He's not smiling anymore, but then who would be?

'That was a pretty smart game you played, Peter,' I say, 'calling me in to look after Leonardo, while you and Paul here made off with the paintings. You nearly got away with it, too.'

Suddenly, click, the lights go out. Something whirrs through the air. I dive for cover. Leonardo starts caterwauling again. The door slams. I jump up and fumble my way to the light switch. I flick it on.

Robin Peter is lying on his back with his

legs in the air and his wings crumpled about him like soggy wafers. There is a growing patch of red across his breast and it's not embarrassment. Sticking in his heart is a small, but deadly arrow. I go over and nudge him with my foot. He's dead as a dodo. I pull a white sheet of paper over his face.

'Now,' I say. 'Who killed this cocky robin?'

But I have no need of a reply. It's obvious really. Think about it. He's done it before, hasn't he? Remember the old rhyme:

Who killed cock robin?

'I,' quoth the sparrow, 'with my bow and arrow...'

Case closed. It's time for me to fly.

Asking
Andrea

Asking Andrea

by Alex Stewart

I've never quite got the hang of Mondays,
and this one starts off worse than most.
I'm just getting off the bike outside the
school gates when Creamy Lewis arrives,
smirking at me through the window of his
dad's BMW as the tyres throw up a shower
of muddy water all over my shoes. (His
name's really Justin, but we call him
Creamy because he's rich and thick.)

'Bit wet, Martin?' he asks, grinning at me, and I shrug as though I don't really care, because I know that'll wind him up far more than telling him what I really think of him and his dad.

'It's raining,' I point out, 'and I'm on a bike. What do you think?'

Some of the girls are passing, and they laugh, which makes Creamy scowl and stomp off to the cloakroom, because when it comes to a battle of wits he's practically unarmed. I squelch over to the bike shed, and my lock won't open, because the 3's worn, and I have to jiggle it about a bit, which means by the time I've got my ride chained up it's well past time for the bell, and I have to leg it.

As it turns out, I needn't have hurried, because the cloakroom's still full of people after all. Most of them are jammed against the walls, because the middle of the room's taken up with a lot of noise and shoving, most of which is coming from Andrea, the best-looking girl in the class. (Actually, she's the best-looking girl in the whole school, town, planet; in fact, the entire universe, probably.) She's clever, too, and really funny, and I'd been trying to ask her to the end of term disco for weeks, but I never quite got the chance.

You know how it is with girls, they're always hanging around with their mates, and if you go anywhere near them they start giggling and nudging each other. I just knew if I asked her in front of them it would be round the whole playground before the end of break that Martin the geek had been blown out by Andrea, and I'd never hear the last of it. And, my luck being what it is, every time I saw her without the coven in tow, *my* mates were hanging around, yakking on about computer games and *Doctor Who*, making me look even nerdier than usual; like any self-respecting girl's going to go out with someone whose friends actually care whether Batman or Spiderman would win if they had a fight. (Spidey, obviously, he'd just jump on the ceiling and splat Batty Boy with webbing, game over. But they belong to different comic companies, so it'll never happen.)

Anyhow, the rest of the noise is coming from Andrea's part-time best friend Bethany, and it seems obvious from the general level of shrieking, and the fact that she's trying to flush Andrea's head down the toilet, that they've fallen out again. This happens about three times a term, on average, although not usually so dramatically; they generally just spend a week or so telling each other they're

not talking every time they meet, sometimes
for hours, until they realise they've forgotten
whatever it was they're hacked off about
anyway, and carry on as if nothing had
happened. I think maybe I ought to try
breaking it up or something, but I'd probably
lose an arm, and the rest of the class wouldn't
appreciate me spoiling the fun, so I ask my
mate Rob what's going on instead.

'Maybe you should ask Creamy,' he says,
grinning, so I look over in his direction, and
he's shuffling his feet, trying so hard to look
as though he's got nothing to do with it
that it must be his fault somehow. 'Bethany
heard him ask Andrea to the disco.'

'So?' I say, trying to pretend I don't feel
as if he's just ripped the cover off my
signed Dan Abnett *Torchwood* novel. 'Why
should she care?'

'Because he took Bethany out for a pizza

at the weekend, and she thinks they're dating,' Rob says, with a touch of envy, because the closest he's ever likely to get to a girl is drooling over the pictures in *Loaded*.

It's still anybody's guess whether Andrea's going to get an Armitage Shanks shampoo, as she's on the gym team and quite muscular for her size, but Bethany's a bit on the chunky side, and she's got a lot of weight behind her. On balance, I'd call it for Andrea, except Miss Bullivant turns up and separates them with a few choice words before we get a chance to find out.

'Detention!' she says. 'Both of you! Not another word!'

And she stands there doing the scary look teachers learn at college, until they've shuffled into the classroom, trying to pretend the other one doesn't exist, which can't be that easy as their desks are butted up together. Everyone else starts filing in too, now the entertainment's over, and I go to hang up my coat and put my cycling helmet in my locker.

As I slam the door, which I have to do just right, as the metal's bent and it just springs open again otherwise, I can see Creamy's locker hasn't shut properly either. He's already gone, scuttling into the classroom in the middle of the crowd, doing his best to be invisible.

I just can't help it. He's a smug, selfish git. He's taking Andrea to the disco. My feet are soaked, and he thinks it's funny. It's payback time.

I prise the locker open, and there, on the floor, are his brand new Nikes. Inspiration strikes. One pair of wet feet deserves another.

I'm just zipping up again, feeling the warm glow of a job well done, when the Hand of Doom falls heavily on my shoulder.

'What on Earth do you think you're doing?' yells Miss Bullivant, in tones of outraged astonishment. 'Detention!'

As luck would have it, by mid morning the sun has broken through, and by lunchtime it's a perfect spring day. As I slouch into detention, I can hear everyone else having a great time outside. Monday's out to get me, all right.

'You're late,' Miss Bullivant says, looking up from her Mills and Boon just long enough to notice my arrival.

'Sorry Miss. There was a big queue in the dinner hall.' Which is actually true, although the main thing holding me up was the number of people who wanted to

43

pat me on the back; Creamy's not exactly Mr Popular. I might just as well have saved my breath, though. Miss Bullivant's well away already, completely lost in her book again.

The only other person in the room is Andrea. She's reading something too, and to my surprise, she looks up and smiles at me. Encouraged, I slip into the seat beside her.

'Where's Bethany?' I ask, keeping my voice down, so as not to spoil Miss Bullivant's story for her. I like to be considerate.

Andrea shrugs.

'Dentist's appointment. Double filling. She always was lucky.'

'Not lucky enough to be going to the disco with Cre— Justin, though,' I say, trying to sound as though I couldn't care less.

'If she doesn't want to, that's her business,' Andrea says, and a sudden flare of hope burns through me.

'I thought he asked you,' I say.

'He did. And if Bethany hadn't flown off the handle like that, she'd have heard me turn him down.' She pulls a face like she's just bitten into a lemon. 'I mean, *Creamy Lewis*? I'm not that desperate.'

She slips a bookmark into the novel she's reading, and closes it, and I can see it's a Terry Pratchett.

'Why would you be desperate?' I ask, not getting it. 'Half the school would jump at the chance to go out with you.'

'I don't want to go out with half the school. Just someone who sees more than a pretty face when he looks at me, and doesn't think I'm weird for liking this stuff.'

She glances at the book in front of her.

'What's weird about the *Discworld* books?' I'm getting well out of my depth by this time. 'They're funny, and clever, and there's much more to them than you'd think.' Then I suddenly realise what I'm saying. 'Like you.'

Andrea goes a funny shade of pink, but on her it looks good. I wait for her to say something. She doesn't, but she seems to be waiting for something too, and after a moment I realise what it is.

'Would you like to come to the disco with me?' I say, bracing myself for the putdown that's bound to follow. It feels as though the world's holding its breath.

'Yes,' she says at last. 'I think I would.'

Mondays, eh? Never have been able to get the hang of them. But sometimes they turn out all right.

A Dish
Best
Served
Cold

A Dish Best Served Cold

by Julia Williams

'Oi, Harry Potter, where's your magic wand?' A paper dart flew over my head as I walked into class on Monday morning with my friend Lizzie. I spun round to see my mortal enemy Kieran Allthwaite grinning at me. As I did so I accidentally tripped over Lizzie's feet, and flew down the classroom on my stomach. It would have been a great move if I'd been breakdancing.

'Loser,' I said, with what remained of my dignity.

'I'm not the one on the floor, Turniphead,' said Kieran with a grin.

I got up stiffly, trying to ignore the hysteria of my classmates and the fact I had chewing gum stuck to my skirt.

'Leave it, Goofboy,' I snarled. 'Or I might tell the whole class about the time you wet yourself at infant school.'

Kieran simply made the 'L' sign at me and my classmates laughed even louder. It's great to start the week knowing you've given pleasure to so many.

'Ooh, so original.' I smiled sweetly at him and sat down with Lizzie. If anyone's a loser it's Kieran. I've known him like forever. Unfortunately our mums bonded over coffee when we were infants. As I

happened to get my amazingly attractive
glasses around the first time we watched
Harry Potter at his house, the name's
stuck. I retaliated with Goofboy when he
got his psychedelic orange train tracks.

Just then the door of the classroom was
flung open and Hazel Carruthers sashayed
in with her chav crew. She is the Queen of
Mean. I swear she's a witch, with her long,
black, spikey hair and purple nail varnish.
She never wears the correct uniform and
no one ever says *anything*. Yet the one time
I shortened my skirt by a measly
centimetre, it was straight into detention
for me. Hazel even has a spooky familiar,
like a witch. Well, OK, it's a rabbit, but it
could mean she's a witch.

Hazel cast a malevolent look at the
back of the class, where we'd gone to sit so
we could pass notes to each other while

Nutty Nora, our drama teacher, showed us *Sweeney Todd*. It is all about this barber who slits people's throats and puts them in pies. It sounds gross. I keep telling Nutty Nora she's going to scar me for life, but she says Sondheim is a genius and it is part of our musical theatre training.

'Hop it,' Hazel said to Kieran. 'Neeks like you shouldn't be sitting in the back.'

'I'm not a neek,' began Kieran (he so is), 'and I can sit where I want—'

'Really?' Andy Parsons marched over. He's nearly a metre taller then the rest of the boys in the class, and nearly as wide. He has a face like a squashed flat bulldog and arms like a gorilla's. Andy fancies the pants off Hazel, so she uses him as her muscle.

It wasn't a pretty fight. Kieran tried to throw a punch, but his fist just bounced off

Andy's fat stomach. Andy grabbed Kieran by the neck and lifted him off the floor. Kieran flailed wildly, but Andy just gave him a pitying smile, before dropping him on the floor like a pathetic maggot. Before Kieran could get up again, he found himself pinned to the back of the classroom, with his nose pressed against the wall and his arm twisted behind his back.

'Where are you sitting?' Andy said.

'*Snorf, snorf*,' said Kieran, but I think he meant: It's ok, I'm moving.

'Let's try this again, shall we?' Hazel smiled dangerously at me. 'You two creeps aren't going to cause us any trouble either, are you?'

Lizzie and I sighed. We didn't want to become punching bags for Andy. We've seen him sit on enough year sevens in the playground. *No one* does that. That's like squishing ants.

'Who's the neek now?' Kieran said to me, as I reluctantly sat down in the only available seat, which happened to be next to him. This day just got better and better.

'I'm no neek,' I said.

'No, you're a geek,' grinned Kieran, like he was being so original.

'And you're a – a –' I searched my brain for a suitable insult and could only come up with 'leek'.

'Loser,' said Kieran.

'Oh be quiet,' I said.

At that moment Nutty Nora came in and started to tell us about *Sweeney Todd*. It sounded even worse than I had imagined. I was all right until she mentioned the B word. I have a fatal weakness. I cannot stand the sight of blood.

'Did you know you've gone green?' said Kieran, looking at me with interest.

'Shut up,' I hissed. I was beginning to feel faintly sick. This was so going to be a film I couldn't watch.

I lasted until the first murder. I stood up to ask to be excused. Then I keeled over. Right there in front of the whole class. Talk about humiliating.

'Told you she was pathetic,' said Hazel so loudly they could probably have heard it on the moon. And yet, miraculously, Nutty Nora didn't. I knew she was a witch.

I sat out the rest of the lesson in the nurse's office, but when I joined the rest of the class for PHSE, it was clear that I had been a hot topic of conversation.

'Ooh, Andy, save me, save me,' Hazel said as I walked back in the classroom. 'I

cut my finger and I can't stand the sight
of blood.'

'Ha, ha,' I said and sat down grumpily.
What did I have to go and faint for? Now
Hazel would never leave me alone.

Soon the whole school knew I'd fainted in
drama. Every time I came into the canteen
people would call: 'Watch out, Vampire
Girl, blood's on the menu today,' or
'What's your next trick going to be,
throwing up in Biology?' (Actually, it
was a close run thing the time they
showed us how babies are born.)
Everyone joined in, even Lizzie.

'What can I do?' she said, when I
protested that as my bezzie she was supposed
to protect me. 'Hazel says she'll tell
everyone that I kissed Joe Spamhead behind
the bikesheds at the last school disco.'

'But you didn't,' I said.

'I know, but I can't afford for my reputation to be ruined for ever,' said Lizzie.

I thought about this for a moment. Joe Spamhead was so geeky, neeky, and leeky he made Kieran look like He-Man. Lizzie would never get a decent boyfriend ever again if word got out she'd kissed him.

'Fair enough,' I said, 'but try not call me a vampire *every* day.'

The only person who didn't tease me was Kieran. This was very weird. He is supposed to tease me. That's like, his *job*. What was going on?

'Fancy getting your own back?' Kieran sidled up to me in our library period. 'Nice to see you're reading something educational.'

I hastily hid my copy of *Mizz* underneath *The Lord of the Rings*.

'It is educational, I'm learning how to cope with being bullied,' I said loftily. 'What do you mean about getting my own back?'

'Oh come on,' said Kieran. 'You must want to get your revenge on Hazel, and I have just the way to do it.'

Accepting that Kieran was being nice to me took some doing. This was the boy who cut the legs off my Barbie when I was six, and tried to flush my head down the toilet when I was eight. But given that no one else was helping me, I couldn't look a gift horse in the mouth.

'OK,' I said, 'suppose I accept this great plan of yours, what's in it for you?'

'Such cynicism in one so young,' sighed Kieran. 'I just want to get Hazel back.'

'So what's the plan, then?' I asked.

'Well, you know Hazel has that dumb lop-eared bunny, Flopsy?'

'I think the whole world knows about Flopsy,' I said. Hazel is devoted to that stupid bunny. She's housetrained it and everything. She even takes it out for walks.

'Did you know she'd lost him?'

As I am now nerd queen of the century and no one talks to me anymore, I didn't know.

'So?' I said.

'So…' Kieran told me his plan, and my eyes widened and I had to suppress a giggle.

'You know that's so stupid it might just work,' I said.

'So we're on?'

'We're on,' I said, 'but you're still a neek.'

'And you're still a loser,' said Kieran.

A week later I was sitting alone in the canteen at school, when Hazel walked past.

'I hear there's a reward out for finding your rabbit,' I said in a loud voice.

'And?' said Hazel. 'What's it got to do with you, Vampire Girl?'

'I think I saw him,' I said.

'Really?' She turned her beady black eyes on me.

'Yes,' I said. 'I'm sure it was Flopsy. I saw him on that patch of wasteground at the back of the school. I can show you after school if you like.'

Hazel still looked suspicious, but she did love that rabbit, so after a moment's indecision, she said, 'OK, I'll meet you. But no funny stuff. Right?'

She marched off, and I had to restrain my

laughter. This was going to be so much fun.

'So where did you see Flopsy?' said Hazel as she and the chav crew picked their way awkwardly in their high heels over the wasteground.

'Well, I think he hopped this way,' I said. I led them through the rubble and pot holes, till we came out on to a street where there was a café where we sometimes hang out.

'I'm sure he went in here,' I said.

I marched into the café, where I found Kieran sitting eating a pie.

'What's that you're eating?' I said, as Hazel came bounding in after me.

'Flopsy-wopsy, coochy-coo? Where are you?' she purred.

'Oh it's the yummiest of pies,' Kieran said, rolling his eyes and making *mmm*,

mmm noises. 'I never knew rabbit could be so tasty.'

Hazel stopped cooing for Flopsy, disbelief registering in her eyes.

'You're never eating rabbit,' she said.

'Kieran didn't get the pie here,' I said. 'We made it.'

'You made it?' Hazel looked incredulous. 'I don't believe you.'

'Yes we did,' said Kieran, smiling a sweet smile. 'I went out to my vegetable patch last night and saw a stupid lop-eared bunny eating all my mum's carrots. So I shot it with my air rifle, and Cassie here put it in a pie. It's really yummy. Don't you want to try some?'

Hazel suddenly looked pale.

'You – you shot a rabbit?' she said. 'What was its name?'

'I don't know,' Kieran seemed to

consider this slowly. 'Oh yes, I *think* the tag said Flopsy.'

'But – but – that's my rabbit's name,' said Hazel and fainted clean away.

When she came round, she found us standing over her laughing at her.

'You didn't really believe that lame story about Kieran shooting your rabbit, did you?' I said.

'You mean, Flopsy is still alive?' Hazel gabbled, her cheeks growing bright pink.

'Of course he is,' I said. 'Does Kieran look like a bunny boiler?'

'What a loser,' said Kieran.

'And a neek,' I said.

'No, surely a geek,' added Kieran.

'Definitely a leek,' I agreed, and we left the café high fiving it.

'I don't think Hazel will be bothering you again,' said Kieran.

I suddenly felt awkward. It still didn't seem right for Kieran to be nice to me.

'Well, um, thank you,' I said. 'But why did you help me? I thought you hated my guts.'

'Of course I do,' said Kieran. 'But someone had to put Hazel in her place. Besides, if anyone gets to call you a loser, it should be me.'

'Well that's rich coming from the biggest neek on the planet,' I said.

'Says the geek,' said Kieran.

'Oh shut up you leek,' I said, 'I think perhaps we've become friends by mistake.'

And I put my arm through his and we walked down the road fighting about which was the best *Doctor Who* episode ever.

Nice to have things back to normal.